Not Fair, Won't Share!

A Pinky and Blue Story

by Lindsey Gardiner

ORCHARD BOOKS

FALKIRK COUNCIL
LIBRARY SUPPORT
FOR SCHOOLS

D0186588

For Corrie

ORCHARD BOOKS
96 Leonard Street, London EC2A 4XD
Orchard Books Australia
Unit 31/56 O'Riordan Street, Alexandria, NSW 2015
ISBN 1 84121 848 0 (hardback)
ISBN 1 84121 106 0 (paperback)
First published in Great Britain in 2001
First paperback publication in 2002
Copyright © Lindsey Gardiner 2001
The right of Lindsey Gardiner to be identified as the author and
illustrator of this work has been asserted by her in accordance
with the Copyright, Designs and Patents Act, 1988.
A CIP catalogue record for this book is available from the British Library.
10 9 8 7 6 5 4 3 2 1 (hardback)
10 9 8 7 6 5 4 3 2 1 (paperback)
Printed in Hong Kong / China

Meet Pinky and Blue.

Pinky is small, pink and very noisy.
Yap! Yap! Yap!
Blue is big, blue and likes peace and quiet.
Shhh!

Yap!
Yap!

Pinky and Blue are the
best of friends –
most of the time!

They eat
together.

But Pinky eats lots…
   sometimes she eats Blue's food too.

Yap!
   Yap!
      Yap!

Oh no, Pinky!

They love to
play together.

But Pinky sometimes runs off
with Blue's bouncy ball.

Yap!
Yap!
Yap!

Oh no, Pinky!

They sleep together.
Yawn!
Zzzz!
Snore!
But sometimes
Pinky can't sleep…

Blue likes having Pinky around and she doesn't mind sharing...

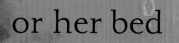

her food
(well, not much)

or her bed

or her rubber ball.

But there's just one thing
        that Blue does NOT share...

SQUISHY RABBIT!
Pinky wants Squishy Rabbit all for herself.

Pinky and Blue tug and tug —

Push! **Woof!** Pull! Yap!
Push! **Woof!** Pull! Yap!

until...

off comes Squishy Rabbit's ear!
Pinky thinks it's funny...

Oh no, Pinky!

but Blue is angry.

"Go away, Pinky," shouts Blue.

"You spoil everything!"

And that's what Pinky did.

Plod!

Plod!

Plod!

All the way to the bottom of the garden.

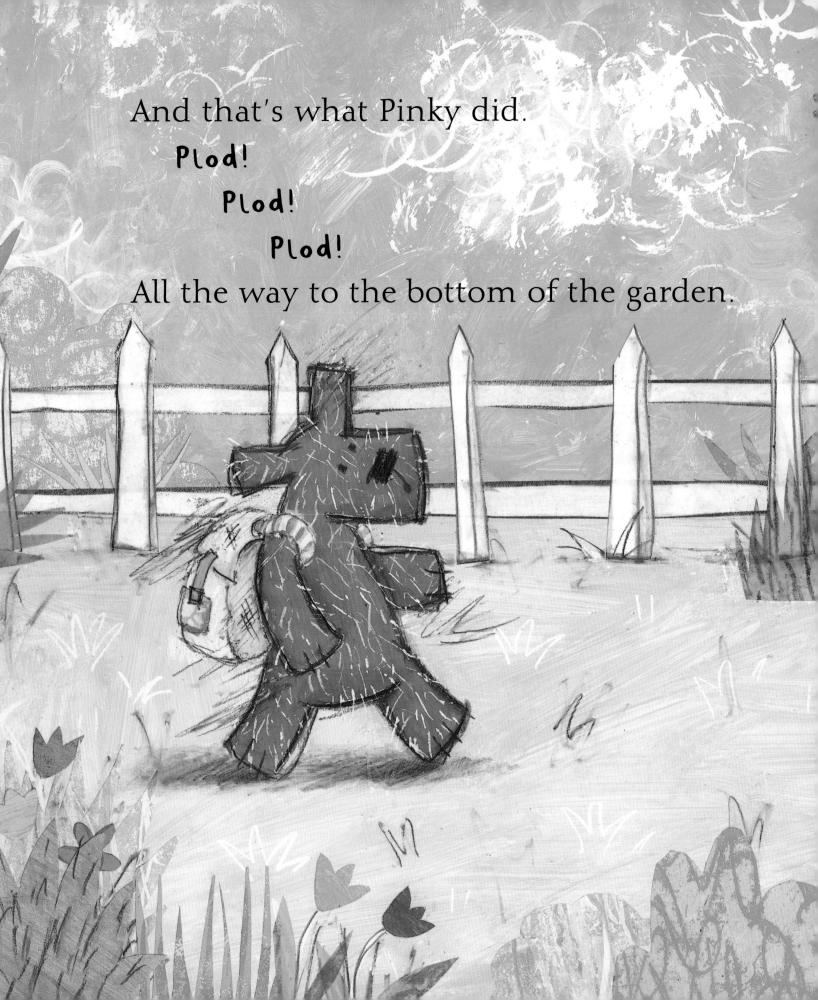

Poor Pinky felt sad,
all alone in the shed.

She was cold
and it was getting dark.

But Blue was happy.

She didn't have to share her toys,

she didn't have to share her food,

she could sleep peacefully and best of all...

Blue had Squishy Rabbit all to herself!

But Blue began to miss Pinky.
She missed Pinky's

Yap!
Yap!
Yap!

She missed Pinky tugging at her tail and
she missed having someone to play with.

Blue missed Pinky...

and Pinky
missed Blue!

So Pinky decided to come back.

She climbed in through the window.

Clunk!

And Blue was very happy to have her home!

Now Pinky still
eats Blue's food.

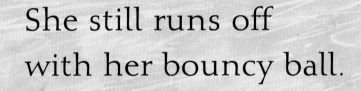

Pinky

Gulp!

Gulp!

Blue

She still runs off
with her bouncy ball.

She still tugs at her tail...

Yelp!

and she is still VERY noisy.

Yap!
Yap!
Yap!

And Blue still shares her food.

She still shares her bouncy ball.

She still shares her bed and

she still likes peace and quiet.

Shhh!

Blue

But Pinky tries not to run off
with Squishy Rabbit anymore,
    and Blue tries not to get angry.

ZZZ
Z
Z

This way they get on really well...

FALKIRK COUNCIL
LIBRARY SUPPORT
FOR SCHOOLS

most of the time!

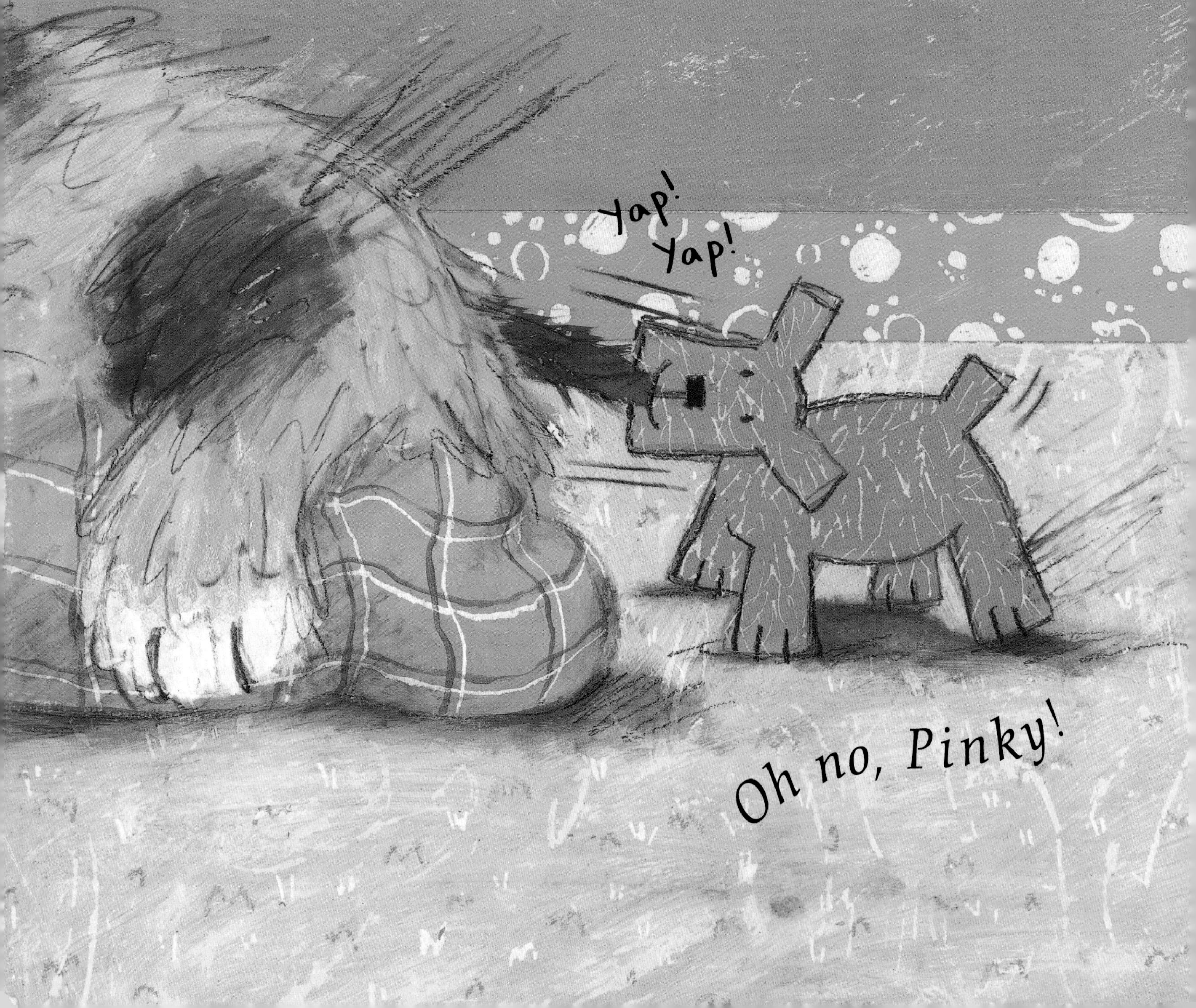

Oh no, Pinky!